our ROOTS

A COLLECTION OF STORIES INSPIRED BY
SEEDFOLKS,
A NOVEL BY PAUL FLEISCHMAN

ESOL 3, GLEN BURNIE HIGH SCHOOL,
2015-2016

ESOL 3, GLEN BURNIE HIGH SCHOOL, 2015-2016

Copyright © 2016 ESOL 3, Glen Burnie High School, 2015-2016

All rights reserved.

ISBN: 1530629551
ISBN-13: 978-1530629558

ESOL 3, Glen Burnie High School, 2015-2016

Table of Contents

Introduction	page 5
Javier	page 6
Swastika	page 12
William	page 18
Cindy	page 22
Adil	page 26
Alex	page 30
Bryan	page 34
Christian	page 38
Hina	page 42
Gaby	page 46
Gildardo	page 48
Humara	page 52
Nabil	page 56
Pedro	page 60
Roha	page 62
Samip	page 66
Shahin	page 70
Ayomide	page 74
Trang	page 76
Truc	page 80
Utsab	page 84
Zoiya	page 86
Cesar	page 90
Rosa	page 94
Kafher	page 98
Edwin	page 102
David	page 104
Carlos	page 108

Acknowledgements

The process of making and writing *Our Roots, A collection of stories inspired by Seedfolks*, was long and arduous and certainly could not have been done single-handedly.

First and foremost we would like to thank our teacher, Ms. Tema Encarnación, who gave us the opportunity to read *Seedfolks* which guided our book. Ms. Encarnación has been unfailingly supportive in editing and organizing our work. Her encouragement to keep going and to keep improving our English skills was key to making our book a success.

We would also like to thank Mr. Paul Fleischman, the author of *Seedfolks*, for being an inspiration to our class. Because of his captivating story, we were able to get inspiration in telling our own stories through his fictional tale.

We would like to express our gratitude to Ms. Kelly Reider, the Anne Arundel County ESOL Coordinator for her encouragement and support in bringing this book into being. Her kind words and ongoing support of our hard work kept us writing and editing, even when things were difficult.

The principal and assistant principal of our school, Ms. Vickie Plitt and Ms. Shelley Hartford, have supported us through the process of getting permissions and wiavers to ensure that our book will make it to publication. We are very grateful for their support on this project.

Finally, we would like to recognize our own contributions in helping one another understand the text as we participated in literature circles during our reading of *Seedfolks*. We supported one another through the writing process and we were strong teammates in making this book become a reality.

Each of us was supported by our families throughout the process and we would like to thank them for the opportunities that they have given us and the lessons they have taught us.

ESOL 3, GLEN BURNIE HIGH SCHOOL, 2015-2016

INTRODUCTION

In the spring of 2016 the ESOL (English for Speakers of Other Languages) 3 classes at Glen Burnie High School read the novel *Seedfolks*, by Paul Fleischman. Fleischman's book tells the story a young girl who honors her father's memory by planting lima beans in an empty lot in her neglected neighborhood. Her one small act of homage profoundly impacts her community.

Throughout our study of *Seedfolks*, students honed their reading skills by annotating the text to more fully comprehend it. They used writing to reflect on themes such as prejudice, teen pregnancy, bias and personal responsibility. Students also used structured classroom routines to engage in meaningful discussions of the text to continue to build their oral and aural language skills.

After reading Fleischman's story, students were inspired to write their own chapters of *Seedfolks*. The following pages tell their stories in an intriguing mixture of fiction and reality. Many of the narratives intertwine the students' own immigration experiences as they came to the United States, tackled a new language and navigated a new culture all set within the fictional neighborhood described in Fleischman's work. Enjoy!

IMAGE BY: REBECCA GILMORE

ESOL 3, Glen Burnie High School, 2015-2016

About Javier

My name is Olvin Javier I was born in Tela Atlantida, Honduras on November 23. My parents are Sonia and Sergio I am the fourth child of my parents. I have 6 siblings in total but one of them is just my half brother. Currently, I devote myself to my studies in Glen Burnie High School.

Earlier in Honduras I finished my elementary and middle school studies. When I left Honduras, I was studying my technical degree in computer science and letters but I couldn't finish because I had to move to the USA. I came to the USA looking for a better opportunity because Honduras is having a hard situation economically and socially. Economically in the sense of a lack of employment due to the lack of help from the government and socially due to the wave of violence in which the country is involved.

Like my mom and dad who had to leave our country and find elsewhere I decided to come to the United States with my brother and prepare myself to help my family.

One of my favorite things is to play the piano but unfortunately I have never put it into practice. Also I like to read and write. I have read a lot of books in Honduras, all of them in Spanish and about different topics

When I came to Glen Burnie High school I knew I would have a lot of obstacles. The first I had to face was the language. I still remember my first day in school. I thought it would be horrible to not understand my classes and I was afraid I would fail them. But it wasn't that bad. I did not know they had a program called ESOL which has helped me a lot.

ESOL 3, GLEN BURNIE HIGH SCHOOL, 2015-2016

I met a lot of people from different countries in that program. I've always given my best in learning English and when I got Mrs Encarnacion's ESOL class, it was awesome for me because we started to read some books. The one that made a connection with me was *Seedfolks* because it talked to us about different types of cultures and people's stereotypes.

There is a chapter in the book that is called Nora which talks about a nurse who tries her best to help Mr Myles. I like this chapter because Mr Myles is a man who doesn't surrender easily. *Seedfolks* is a very interesting book that inadvertently makes a connection with me and my life.

TO HEAR THE CHAPTER READ BY THE AUTHOR, SCAN THE QR CODE OR USE THE LINK BELOW.

tinyurl.com/javierschapter

ESOL 3, GLEN BURNIE HIGH SCHOOL, 2015-2016

Javier's Chapter

I have always been with my siblings. We were inseparable. But when my mom and dad left us and went to look for better opportunities in others countries, my dad in Cleveland and my mom in Pamplona, Spain, my affectionate family started to fall apart. I expected it and I was not surprised. If you have lived in Honduras you can understand why. I have seen so many families fall apart that it does not surprise me anymore. I still remember when my brother, who lives in Cleveland, asked me if I wanted to go to live with him. Even though I did not agree, I had to do it. What happens when you do not have opportunities and finally you get one? You will take it. Even when it is not specifically what you were expecting to have. That was exactly what happened to me. I decided to come with my brother and find better opportunities. I thought that saying goodbye to my loving family was the worst thing I had to face.

But my first week in Cleveland was worse than I thought. In a place where the language is different, believe me, it is as if you do not exist in that place. I asked my brother how could I get by in a place where I do not know any of my neighbors. He answered me " we are not surviving we are adapting ourselves." I still was confused because how will I get by if I can not even survive. Without a doubt I was not comfortable in Cleveland. It is a big change starting from the weather and continuing on with the culture. There was something that made me interested in being there, though. It was a garden, my brother had been talking to me sometimes about it, but because it was winter I hadn't gone to see it.

Until one day we had a snowstorm. I hadn't seen that much snow in my life. The first hours were fantastic until it became uninteresting. Finally the snowstorm stopped and my brother and I finally came out after two days. It was a mess, the whole garden was covered with snow, and finally I saw everyone who lives in Cleveland.

But each person was cleaning their own area in the garden. When my brother and I were done with our garden I saw an old woman with an old man shoveling the snow that their garden had. The first impression I had of them was of my grandparents. I asked my brother if he wanted to go and help them. I was nervous because that was my first time I talked to my neighbors. I said "Hello" and ask them if we could help them.

They kindly said, "Absolutely yes." The old woman asked me my name and I told her my name and I requested her name too. She said "My name is Nora" and he is my friend Mr. Myles. Finally, I was talking with one of my neighbors! I couldn't pass up the opportunity and asked them what they had planted before the snowstorm. They said they had some apples. Mrs. Nora talked to me about how they have been working and asked me if I would like to be a part of the garden and what I would plant. I thought about my siblings and their favorite kinds of fruits which were grapes. I came back from my thoughts and I told her if I just could have a little part of a garden I would plant grapes because that reminds me of my siblings and all those fun times I had with them.

Mrs. Nora smirked me and told me, "Because you have given me an intriguing answer, now you have a part of our garden, now you can plant anything you would like." Trust me I was so ecstatic.. Finally I was getting comfortable in Cleveland. The next day I woke up early and I got ready to plant my grapes in the garden. After some days, finally, I was seeing how my grapes were growing up very healthy.

When Mrs. Nora saw my plants, she told me, "I know how proud you feel Javier, no one else but me can understand why," she said with a smile on her face. "I left my country and also my family too. Before my family was British. When I left England I was just a teenager, I came here for the same reason you did. A better opportunity. But that can only happen if you decide to make roots. Only then will you have a delicacy of fruits." From that moment Mrs.

Nora taught me an important lesson, I still remember Mrs Nora's phrase, "What you sow is what you reap." I started to think that maybe I was complaining too much and realized that people become only become friendly with you if you are friendly with them. All that Mrs. Nora said to me has helped me to change my thinking of my neighbors through the garden.

ESOL 3, GLEN BURNIE HIGH SCHOOL, 2015-2016

IMAGE BY: TEMA ENCARNACION

ESOL 3, Glen Burnie High School, 2015-2016

ABOUT SWASTIKA

My name is Swastika. I am from the small and beautiful country of Nepal, in Asia. When my brother was born he was blind. In 2007 my dad, mom, and my brother came to the United States for treatment of my brother. I was seven years old when they left. My brother got good opportunities to help him with his blindness.

In August, 2015 I came to the United States. When I arrived in the airport I cried because I was reunited with my mom and dad after eight years. But I didn't see my brother on that first day because he had gone to summer camp. I missed my brother so much. When I got off the airplane I was so happy that finally, I was with my parents.

I came to Glen Burnie High School on September 19, 2015. This school is so big and has so many students. The first day of school was so nice. Teachers and students were so nice to me.

In my ESOL class I read the book called *Seedfolks* in which there is the chapter called Nora. Nora is a nurse who took care of Mr. Myles. She used to take Mr. Myles around the garden in the wheelchair. That chapter relates to my own life because when I was in my country I used to take my great grandfather around the garden in the wheelchair. That chapter reminds me of my great grandfather. When I took my great grandfather to the garden I felt so proud because I was able to walk with him and he was 92 years old. He really loved me a lot. He used to live in the village and one day when he heard that I was sick he didn't think anything of it and came to meet me. I was so happy about it. Even though he is not in this world anymore he is in every one's heart. And he is in my heart. I really miss him. And when I read the chapter of *Seedfolks* I felt so happy to think of my great grandfather.

ESOL 3, Glen Burnie High School, 2015-2016

After he passed away I missed him a lot and that chapter reminds me of him. I really miss my country, my family members and my friends.

Image by: Swastika

To hear the chapter read by the author, scan the QR code or use the link below.

tinyurl.com/swastikaschapter

Swastika

I used to stay with my grandparents in my country. My parents moved to the United States when I was seven years old for the medical eye checkup of my brother. He is blind but so talented in other ways. I missed my parents so much. I used to enjoy living with my grandparents and cousins. When we had vacations I used to go tour with my cousins to explore my country, Nepal, which is full of natural resources and natural beauties like mountains, rivers, and lakes. I used to spend most of my time with my dog, Sweetu in the garden. He is so cute and I loved him a lot. Even though I was far from my parents, my relatives really loved and cared for me a lot.

When I became older I always cried when I missed my parents and I got some negative thoughts about my parents. In 2015 an earthquake occurred in our country because of which I was really afraid. I became so sad and because of that it hampered my studies too. My grandparents said to my dad, "you should start the immigration process for your daughter, nowadays she is not so happy." I said to myself, "Finally, after eight years I can see my parents again." I came to the United States on August 10, 2015. When I was at the airport all my relatives came to the airport for me. I was really happy because after a long time I was going to see my parents. When I saw my mom and dad I started crying. But I missed my brother because he had gone to summer camp. I was happy because I met my parents after a long time and also because I was free from the dangerous earthquakes. But I really missed my grandparents, relatives and my cute pet, Sweetu. When I came to the United States we went to Cleveland where my mom and dad have an apartment. They moved from Maryland to Cleveland for better schools for us.

We lived in a neighborhood where there were some problems which were really hard to solve. In my opinion, a neighborhood is a place where people live together and help each other with their problems. But we lived in that community where there were many problems which were difficult to solve and understand. Even though there were not the tough problems it was difficult to solve because the people were not understanding each other. Even though they have some problems they didn't tell us because we were new in the community and they were really nice to me.

    The next day, I got up and got dressed. I told my mom that I would like to hang around the apartment to explore something new. So, I left my room and walked along the sidewalk. I saw a garden which was really nice. And there I found many people taking care of it and surrounding it with a fence. I was walking around when I saw the garden which looked really pretty. Different kinds of plants in the garden looked like different kinds of flowers in a garland.

    I returned home and I asked my mom, " There is such a nice garden, can I plant something over there?" She was like, "Okay!" And she was pretty curious about what I was going to grow in the garden. At that time I wanted to grow some bitter gourd for the memory of my great grand father. He suffered from blood pressure and he often ate that. Even though I didn't liked that vegetable, I used to eat that for my grand father. I really missed him a lot.

    The next day, when I was walking around I met Leona in the garden. I said ,"Hi." She said, "Hi, are you new here?" I said , "Yes." And she said, "I am Leona, nice to meet you." There were some conversations between us. I was really curious about the people in this neighborhood and I asked her some questions about it. She was a really brave person. She said to me that she solved the problem of garbage in the garden by taking a garbage bag in the middle of the meeting in the government office.

    Time was passing and I was late to plant in the garden. I said to her, "Bye, I gotta go now. I have some plants to plant in the garden. So, talk to you later." She said, "Okay! Bye, talk to you later." After that I went to the garden.

I planted the bitter gourd in the garden. First I dug the soil and put some seeds there and watered them and took care of them. It grew really nicely. There was no problem till then. There were so many flowers growing. And the next morning when I went to check on my vegetables there was nothing there. I was shocked. I thought that my mom had already taken them so I went home and asked her about it. She said that she hadn't. I realized that there is a thief who stole my vegetables and that was from our apartment. I discussed it with my neighbors too. I started to doubt one person and I pointed at him. I thought that the people of this apartment were cheap and they stole the stuff of other people.

But, the next day I saw one new unknown person in the garden taking all the vegetables from the garden. I screamed and yelled at him and all the people around the apartment. I asked all the people if someone knew that person but I was shocked. No one knew it it was. I knew that that was the person who stole my bitter gourd. I felt so sorry and guilty because I accused the wrong person as a thief. And other people also said that he is the person who stole the stuff from the garden and there was a misunderstanding among the people because of it. I said sorry to all the neighbours and felt really guilty. They were nice to me and we all decided that there would be a security system in our neighborhood.

After that we took that thief to the cops. We all were really happy because the main problem of our neighborhood was gone. We all enjoyed a lot and were really happy about it. We decided to organize a party and we were all excited.

I learned an important lesson from my neighborhood and this garden. The garden is the memory of the neighborhood and neighbors are needed and important to everyone. Neighbors are the one who help in every place. And the important thing I learned was the importance of neighbors and community.

ESOL 3, GLEN BURNIE HIGH SCHOOL, 2015-2016

IMAGE BY: ROHA

ABOUT WILLIAM

    Currently a student in Glen Burnie High School, I grew up having a background in the cultures of both El Salvador and the United States. My parents are Digna and Carlos, I have one brother whose name is also Carlos. I migrated to the United States to work and continue my studies. The reason I came to the United States was to improve my living conditions and also to help my family to have a better life. Currently living in Glen Burnie MD, I came to live here because of the school and to have more opportunities. I still remember my first day in Glen Burnie High School. It was awful because I did not know anybody here. But soon when I started to know people I felt a little bit better because I had people to talk to now.

    Seedfolks is a book that we read in our ESOL 3 class and it's about how a neighborhood created a garden to get to know each other. Mr. Myles was helped by a woman called Nora. She was a nurse and she was helping him so he could speak again. My experience seems like Mr. Myles in *Seedfolks* because he needed a wheelchair and he couldn't speak because he lost his ability to talk so he couldn't talk to anyone. One day Nora took him on a walk and three blocks down from his apartment they saw a garden and Mr Myles felt something special because he knew how to plant so he felt he was a part of the garden. This was same as me. I was feeling a little bit bad because I wasn't able to talk with anybody because of the language barrier and the also because I did not know anybody. Soon when I started to hang out with friends and get to know them I felt better because at least I had friends now.

    Something that impacted me the most in *Seedfolks* was how a community can change or build a good relationship within the neighborhood. At first it was only one person, Kim. She was the one who started the garden but then more people came in to join them and help to build the garden.

ESOL 3, GLEN BURNIE HIGH SCHOOL, 2015-2016

WILLIAM'S CHAPTER

It was a lovely afternoon when my charming family and I were in an appealing beach called, "El Cuco." It was an amazing day, the sun was brighter than ever, the splendid birds were flying above the beach, a lot of people were walking around the place. It was just an amazing day. Until my father called us to have a mini-reunion to speak about something. At first I thought it wasn't important, but once my father started to speak about what he wanted to tell us I knew it was something bad. He started off by saying that we knew how the situation in our homeland was and that we must need to immigrate to the United States. When my father said that, I felt like I was leaving behind all my childhood and everything I had. But I also knew it was for the best. Three days later we arrived in a town called Cleveland, escaping from our dangerous homeland because of the violence and gangs there.

My father had some friends in Cleveland. That is why my father decided to come here. At first I felt like it wasn't a place for me because I did not know anybody. One day I went to take a walk around the neighborhood to get to know my neighbors and the place a little bit better. Three blocks down from my apartment I saw a wonderful garden where there were a lot of people planting and it got my attention. I went over to see what was happening there. Once I got there I met Royce who was always walking around cheerfully in the impressive garden. At first I was shy because I didn't know anyone in the garden but then Royce came over where I was standing and he started to talk to me saying, "Hey new guy, what is your name?" I wasn't sure if I had to tell him my name so I made up a name and I told him my name was Alcides.

He looked like a bad person, but after a few minutes he showed me all around the garden and I thought it was incredible because all the people came together in the garden. But I didn't know why all the people were staring at us with a rough look. Royce left me a block away from the garden. Then I wondered why they stared at us like that. I went back and I saw a guy named Curtis who was planting beautiful tomatoes and I asked him why they stared at us like that. He said it was because of Royce. He told me they didn't like him at all. I asked him, "Why? Because Royce told me he loves the garden and he is always taking care of it.

ESOL 3, Glen Burnie High School, 2015-2016

I thought that was the first problem in the neighborhood. Just because he looks like he is a bad person doesn't mean he actually is one. Then I went back to my apartment with a joyful feeling because I found some friends in the neighborhood. The other day I went back to the garden and Curtis was there. I asked him why he was planting tomatoes and he responded to me saying that he was planting tomatoes for his girl and I asked him why. He said it was because he wanted her back because they were mad at each other. After that he said, "Hey why don't you plant something in the garden?" At first I wasn't sure about it but then I thought if Curtis is planting tomatoes for his girl, I can plant anything I want to remember my country.

I decided to plant daisies and olives because daisies mean "faith" and olives mean "peace". I thought about my country. All I wanted was that my country could find peace and faith. After a week my daisies and olives were growing so brightly and beautifully. At the end of the month my plants were so pretty and taller than the others in the garden. I thought about it for a second and realized that the garden was helping me to get through everything and it was because of my daisies and olives. This changed my point of view about the garden and also the neighborhood because I felt like I was a part of the garden since my plants were so pretty and taller than the others.

I thought about my country and the garden and I learned that even though you are not in your country you can remember it and also wish them the best. That is why I planted my daisies and olives because I was hoping maybe by doing this it would help my country to get better and my faith was so immense that that could happen.

To hear the chapter read by the author, scan the QR code or use the link below.

tinyurl.com/williamschapter

ESOL 3, GLen Burnie HIGH SCHOOL, 2015-2016

image By: Bryan

ESOL 3, GLEN BURNIE HIGH SCHOOL, 2015-2016

ABOUT CINDY

My name is Cindy and I was born in Santa Barbara, Honduras. I'm 19 years old. My parents are Maria and German. Fiorela is my older sister and Joshua my younger brother. I also have a niece named Ashley. I came from Honduras for many reasons but one of them is that my dad lived in the United States for almost 13 years. I immigrated to the United States because in Honduras there is a lot of crime and not many job opportunities. I think God has a purpose for me here. I believe that God's plans are much better than mine. I believe in God.

I came to Glen Burnie High School because my dad had his job near Glen Burnie, MD and Glen Burnie High School was a good option for me because they have an ESOL program to learn English. It is a great opportunity for all immigrant students who wish for a better future. My first days in Glen Burnie were good because I spent time with my dad and my brother who was born in the United States. I was excited to see the United States but even more for being with my family. On the other hand I was unhappy for leaving my mother and my older sister in Honduras. I felt strange in my school and I thought nobody spoke Spanish. Later I met people from El Salvador, Puerto Rico, Guatemala and from many other countries. Those guys were nice and helpful to me.

I read *"SeedFolks"* by the author Paul Fleischman in my ESOL 3 class. My great teacher, Ms.Encarnacion brought the book and I relate to the first chapter of the story about Kim when she made a garden in honor of her dad because she had no memories of him. Since she knew that her dad liked gardens she did made one to make him proud of her. I know how important a dad is because I have fun memories with my own father. I think that family is a significant part of our lives.

Maricela, another character from *Seedfolks* is not happy about being pregnant. She dropped out of high school and wants her body to miscarry her baby. She learned a good life lesson in the garden. One day, Maricela and Leona, another character in the book, have a chat that has a huge impact on Maricela. Maricela changed her mind because Leona showed her that she's part of nature and I think later she started to love her baby. This event impacted me because Maricela finally learned an important lesson from the bad moments or bad decisions that she made.

ESOL 3, GLEN BURNIE HIGH SCHOOL, 2015-2016

CINDY'S CHAPTER

I'm a typical girl who loves baleadas, pupusas and all Hispanic food. I'm joyful and I think the main reason is that I am Honduran. I left my poor house because my dad got a new job in Cleveland. Honduras had criminals but we also have great natural resources.

Here in Cleveland everything looks contaminated, messy and polluted around my new home. Another reason that my family and I left Honduras was because of Hurricane Mitch. Actually, my new community looks the same but I do not think a natural disaster happened here. I think all my neighbors are nasty, lazy and uncaring people because this is an unsafe and unhealthy place for both the children and the adults. Last night I saw a rat running slowly beneath my bed and I was afraid. This place is dark.

Ana, the new friend of my mom gossips and is old. I think she's forty-nine years old. She's seen as angry and mom said that Ana lived over in Cleveland Heights for eighteen years, basically my sister's age. Fiore, my older sister, saw sirens and people killing each other. I hate this violent place. Fiore met a new friend, though. I think her name is Kimberly but my sister called her Kim. Last Sunday we went to Kim's garden. Honestly, I was curious about why and how she made a little garden. Then on the way to the store, again we saw the garden and I wondered the same thing. About 10 minutes Kim was right in the same shop buying rice for her mom. I thought that the time was perfect to clarify my doubts. The first thing I asked was " Hi, how are you Kimberly?" she laughed because I do not speak much English but I always took classes in English. Fiore asked Kim if she could show us her garden. My neighbor Kim is a friendly girl, smart, pale and has small eyes. She does not speak Spanish, her first language is Vietnamese. Kim said that she made the garden in honor of her dad. A better idea is to plant carrots and tomatoes for my family who actually doesn't have much food.

ESOL 3, Glen Burnie High School, 2015-2016

The next morning we went to the garden and we saw trash. Fiore and my brother said "we have to pick up all of the trash. I was tired of trying to clean this dirty place and pick up trash. But later we saw some prisoners helping us, that was weird because it's unusual to see prisoners with chains cleaning trash. I saw a lot of black prisoners, I was scared because I used to think that black people were bad. But now I changed my mind. Those prisoners are good. They picked up and cleaned the garden. I learned an important lesson in the garden. No matter how people see you, your feelings or attitudes say a thousand words and you cannot judge people because you may need help from that person.

To hear the chapter read by the author, scan the QR code or use the link below.

tinyurl.com/cindyschapter

ESOL 3, Glen Burnie HIGH SCHOOL, 2015-2016

ABOUT ADIL

My name is Adil and I was born in India. I am a 19 years old and my religion is Islam. I came from India because I did not like school there because most of the teachers are lazy. Sometimes they do not teach well. That's why my whole family came to the US.

When I came to the USA I lived first in Pennsylvania because my dad's family lived there. But when my family left Pennsylvania my dad and my uncle did not have jobs. After 3 months my family left Pennsylvania to go to Glen Burnie, Maryland because one of my uncles live in Maryland and he said there were a lot of jobs That's why we moved to Glen Burnie.

My first day in Glen Burnie was so exciting. When I came Glen Burnie everything was new. But one thing I did not like was when I went outside I missed my friends because I didn't make any friends.

ADIL'S CHAPTER

I really miss my country. After I moved I didn't like to leave my country but I wanted to make my future. I can not live alone in my country because it is so scary to live by myself in my village. When you live in city you are not scared because it is safe. But my family lived in a small village. When I left my country I missed my cousins and friends.

Do you know why I left my country? Because in my country education is not good. All the schools are bad. Not all, but most teachers don't care about your grades. They take your money after you come to school and they don't care because they already took your money. That's why my mom and dad didn't want me to go to these schools.

That's why I moved to Cleveland. When I started school in Cleveland Heights everybody looked at me and I introduced myself to the class. I told them my name and where I am from. I said, " My name is Adil, I am from India." The first week I didn't like it because everything changed. The air, the water, and even the taste of the food were different. After one week I liked the school and education but I didn't like the neighborhood because everything was dirty and nobody wanted a clean ground, garden or house. Everything was dirty.

One day I went outside with my family for dinner. When I went with my family outside I saw a garden and all the people in the garden. I stayed there a few minutes to see all the people and what they were doing. They were growing plants.

One day I met Maricela. When I met her I felt very happy and we talked to each other. When I asked her she gave me advice. She told me about plants and she told me the benefits of plants. How plants can help you. We are asked each other how we came here.

One day I thought I wanted to do something so I grew cucumbers. Because they make money if you sell them because everyone likes them to use in a salad. When I grew cucumbers in my garden my plants thrived. Some people grew plants with me and their plants died. My plants thrived because Maricela knew about plants and she told me some things about how to take care of plants and to water them.

When my plants thrived then they changed the neighborhood and everybody cleaned and everybody went to the garden and played games. When the garden and neighborhood changed for the better, I felt good because the kids went to the garden and they played games. When we grew the plants then my neighbors started to grow plants too.

I learned so much from this lesson. The first time I learned about good relations between neighbors. All the plants made money for me. I learned a lot from this experience.

To hear the chapter read by the author, scan the QR code or use the link below.

tinyurl.com/adilschapter

ESOL 3, GLEN BURNIE HIGH SCHOOL, 2015-2016

image by: swastika

ESOL 3, GLEN BURNIE HIGH SCHOOL, 2015-2016

ABOUT ALEX

My name is Alejandro and I was born in Oregon but I lived in Mexico for fourteen years. I came to Glen Burnie, Maryland because some of my relatives live in Glen Burnie. I am very friendly and I like meeting new people.

I started to work at a Mexican restaurant two months after I started school in Glen Burnie High School. My first day I was afraid because I didn't understand English and I thought differently about school. In my first day I saw there were a lot of Hispanic students from different countries. I liked the school but sometimes I feel alone because none of my family is here. They are in Mexico Each day I try to be better.

In my ESOL class at Glen Burnie High School I read a book called *Seedfolks*. In each chapter I read about different people and about their lives and when they moved to the U.S. In each chapter everyone talked about their garden and why they created the garden. I relate my life with Sae Young's chapter in *Seedfolks* because I think that we have something in common. When we came here to the U.S. she was independent like me since her husband died and she was left alone.

ALEX'S CHAPTER

When I moved here to Cleveland Heights I left my alluring family in Mexico. I moved here because I wanted to learn different things. My neighborhood in Cleveland has great people. Sometimes I feel alone because none of my family is with me but the people around me in Cleveland help me.

Every afternoon I walk to a place near my house. One day when I was walking I found an abandoned lot. I wondered if I should plant a garden. I could do a good area with a lot of plants. When I went back I asked my neighbors if they wanted to help to make a beautiful place. When I went back to the place I carried three orange trees. Oranges are one of my favorite fruits, and when it is tall, the plant is beautiful.

I had a friend named Leona. She told me about one of my favorite orange trees. I could use the green leaves to make tea when I get a cold if I take it at night and get better. My plants grew very quickly. I went there and I put water on my plants and I moved the dirt to make it. Two of my three orange trees grew very fast.

I was so happy because I believed I was going to get oranges. Some of my neighbors sometimes helped me when I carried water and I took my shovel to dig when it was necessary. They helped me because I told them about my leaves. We could make tea when we are sick if we don't have any medicine. I think it is why a lot of my neighbors helped me because it is a good idea if you have plants that can help the people. Now when my neighbors come to my garden they bring new ideas about some plants that we can use when we are sick. I think it is great if we keep the garden, and if we try to do a big garden with a lot of different plants that are going to help us.

When I planted my orange trees, I planted them because I wanted to get fruit. But I met Leona and she told me something that I could do with my leaves. I could make tea, when I get a cold. I never believed that orange leaves could be used for making tea, now I want to plant more plants to get a big garden that can help us.

TO HEAR THE CHAPTER READ BY THE AUTHOR, SCAN THE QR CODE OR USE THE LINK BELOW.

tinyurl.com/alexschapter

ESOL 3, GLEN BURNIE HIGH SCHOOL, 2015-2016

Image by: Swastika

ABOUT Bryan

My name is Bryan I was born in El Salvador and I'm 18 years old. I feel I'm somebody who makes new friends and I like to make jokes with my friends. In El Salvador I had many friends. When I moved to the United States I was 15 years old. I lived with my grandma before I came here. But in the United States I have 2 sisters and one brother that were born in the United States. My life in El Salvador was so different compared with my life in the United States because in the United States there are many rules at home. I came to live in the Unites States because my family lives in Glen Burnie. I remember my first day in Glen Burnie. I saw my mom after 9 years. I cannot describe that feeling. It was like the happiest moment because I saw my mother and I saw my brother for the first time.

In my ESOL class at Glen Burnie High School I read a story I can relate with my life. The name of the book is *Seedfolks*. That book is about an ugly city with crime, drugs dealers and ,trash in the street's. In the book is a chapter that is different than the others because I feel it has connection with my life. It is about a girl named Kim who is from Vietnam. She made an altar for her dad who died. Kim and her family weres so sad about it. In my case my grandma is not dead but everybody in my family is sad because she is sick and we miss her so much. I have an altar in my heart with everything she taught me. Something that impacted me from *Seedfolks* is the whole book and how it teaches the lesson that if we work together we can have a better community even though everybody has a different story in their lives and everybody is different from others.

ESOL 3, GLEN BURNIE HIGH SCHOOL, 2015-2016

Bryan's Chapter

If you are Salvadoran probably you are friendly like me. I'm friendly to everyone. I don't mind talking to anybody. I mean I like making new friends from other countries. I remember when I was in El Salvador I was living with my grandma. I miss her so much. I lived with her for 14 years and now I'm 18 so it's been four years since I left El Salvador. No matter how hard it is for me to be in a new country or live with my mother it's very different than living with my grandma. There are too many rules here.

I don't have friends and I can't be friendly because I don't speak much English. I live in Cleveland Heights. It's as ugly as a trash here, there are gangsters and people get shot in the street. It's not a good place to live. One day I decided to walk around because maybe I could find somewhere good to go in the afternoon. I walked a lot and I went home because it was too dark outside. I got frustrated because Cleveland is not a place for me.

The next morning I cooked my breakfast because I was alone and then I decided to walk again. That day I found a garden and I saw a lot of people planting in it. There were a lot of diverse people in just one place. There were Asians, African Americans and Mexicans. Or rather, Latinos because here people say all Latinos are Mexicans. I don't mind or I try to not care too much care about it but sometimes it is annoying.

Back in the garden that day I just walked around. I didn't even know anyone from the garden I saw space that nobody was using. I was close to an Asian girl who I guess is shy because she didn't talk to anybody. I was trying to be friendly but she didn't answer me. She just kept putting water on her beans. Later I was tired of walking and I just walked back to my home. I told my mom about the garden and how different the city looks with the garden. My mom didn't agree with me about planting in the garden. She thought it is too dangerous for me because people are mean and they fight with each other. The next day I was thinking all day about the garden and that Asian girl.

I walked back to the garden with some corn that I bought in the store for planting. I didn't buy too much because it is just a for small space I started planting. I remembered my grandma was a farmer with my grandpa. I planted because I wanted to remember them. I was so excited to start my planting of corn. Probably it was a bad idea because my mom would be angry at me. Anyways, my plants took like 7 days to start growing. I don't know how but when my mom saw the garden she loved it too! I was planting just as my grandparents did! The next day I saw the Asian girl crying and I asked her about what happened. She said, "I'm sad because I'm missing my father. It has been a long time since he died." I said "I'm missing my grandparents because I have a long time in the United states."

We started being friends that day. We have a lot of things in common like our families were farmers. That day I made my first friend and that's how Cleveland changed for me.

To hear the chapter read by the author, scan the QR code or use the link below.

tinyurl.com/Bryanschapter

ESOL 3, Glen Burnie High School, 2015-2016

image by: Swastika

ESOL 3, GLEN BURNIE HIGH SCHOOL, 2015-2016

ABOUT CHRISTIAN

My name is Christian and I was born and raised in the Philippines until I moved to the United States. I attend Glen Burnie High School and eventually will graduate in 2019. Living in the United States has provided me with opportunities to grow and develop, both in my personal and academic life.

The reason we moved to the United States was that my family wanted the whole family together. My father and my siblings traveled without my mother. I do not know s the reason to go without our mother. The one who decided to live in Glen Burnie, Maryland was my father. He needed help from his family who live in Glen Burnie.

My first day in Glen Burnie was tiring and exciting because of the flight and traveling to new places. We had arrived at the house and then went to a buffet. The food there was exquisite. It was 2012 when we arrived. I did not know that I have so many relatives.

The book *Seedfolks*, is about a tough neighborhood in Cleveland, Ohio. There is a vacant lot filled with refuse and infested with rats. The story starts off with a little girl who plants a seed in the ground and then strangers got inspired to plant their chosen crop. In the process, they discover the amazing gift of community.

In Sam's chapter, Sam wanted the whole neighborhood to be happy but it did not turn out well. Sam's chapter emotionally impacted me because I also want my family to be happy but it also did not turn out well. It went unhappily because I sometimes respond back to older people and behave contrary to what they believe is right.

Christian's Chapter

Sometimes you don't want to go but you have to. I moved to Cleveland Heights and I don't know where the heck I am. My weary parents have rented an unsightly apartment. My timid self didn't want to enter it. I was too picky. I was living happily in the Philippines, but a chaotic disaster arose. The ground shook vigorously, it was like falling pieces of a Jenga game.

Being destitute was harsh, I didn't like it. This savage neighborhood didn't make me wanna go outside, like the Korean old woman in my neighborhood. Every part of the neighborhood sickens me, dirty trash bags left behind. So dirty it almost makes me want to burn it but I can't play with fire. Someday I can get out of this prison. The outside is violent and unfriendly. I had no one to talk to except my family. There were a theft, no water resources, and too much garbage in the lot. I went to look out of the window and I saw a woman holding a garbage bag, it was unusual to see. Seven hours later, guys with orange suits with distinct numbers on their backs and police picked up the garbage.

The next day, I went to the second floor of the building and I saw two people, a woman and a disabled old man, looking at something from the window. I went down for a minute to get water because I felt dehydrated. I went back and the two vanished. I attempted to go to their recent spot, because of my curiosity on what they were looking at. I saw people-gardening. I began to question myself. Should I plant something?

I went to the garden and planted some strawberries to impress my exhausted mother and father. Strawberries are delightful to eat, especially with whipped cream. I'd properly take care of them and they grew how I expected.

I harvested my strawberries and put them in a small bowl. They didn't fit at all, so I had to give them to someone. Then I saw a Chinese girl. I talked to her and she said, "I appreciate your kindness!" I gave her four strawberries. I become friends with her. We talked, worked, and had fun together. I was wrong that I called her a Chinese girl, she is from Vietnam. She eventually asked me to help her get water. I helped her. While we were coming back from getting water, I got weary and I needed a break. She walked continuously. After five minutes, I got up on my feet and started walking. I saw Kim and an old man, not the old man who is disabled. I placed the water she needed beside where she places her water. I had to leave because the sky was getting darker.

The next day, I went to my garden and took care of my other unripe strawberries. It began to rain. All the people rushed to the awning. People were bumping me everywhere. I almost slipped next to the pregnant woman. Fortunately I didn't. All the people didn't fit. I had to shout to tell them that we needed to work together in order to fit. People listened and followed my instructions, regardless of age. After ten minutes, we fit.

People worked together instead of fighting for space. I changed my view of the neighborhood. I felt proud and happy. There are plenty of ways to solve such a problem.

To hear the chapter read by the author, scan the QR code or use the link below.

tinyurl.com/christianschapter

ESOL 3, GLEN BURNIE HIGH SCHOOL, 2015-2016

IMAGE BY: SWASTIKA

ESOL 3, GLEN BURNIE HIGH SCHOOL, 2015-2016

ABOUT Hina

My name is Hina. I am from India. I'm came here in February 2014. I came here for my studies. Because in my country there is not good education. When I came here, first I lived in Pennsylvania and studied in Methacton High School. There I felt so alone because I had no friends and I couldn't speak English and I didn't understand English.

But after some time me and my family came here to Glen Burnie, Maryland. In Pennsylvania my mom and dad had no jobs. My mom and dad couldn't speak English and they couldn't understand English. So that's why we are came to Glen Burnie. Now my mom and dad understand English.

In ESOL class we read a book named *Seedfolk* in that book is a chapter named Wendell and Wendell was working in the garden. He picked and poured the water slowly in the garden. That reminds me of my family and friends. Because when I was in India me and my friends to the garden every Sunday and we picked flowers. When I read Wendell's chapter I was felt so sad because I really missed my country and friends.

Hina's Chapter

In India I have a big family and many friends. I moved to America in February, 2014. When I came here I had no friends, I felt so alone. But when I started school and I had some friends I started to have fun with new friends. I have a big family in America. But I really missed my Indian family and friends so I went to the garden in my neighborhood with my new friends. We grew some plants but when I came here at first I had no friends and I hadn't seen a garden or plants. After some time I was going to the mall, stores, park, and every Sunday I went to the park and for walks. When I was walking in the park there was a small garden. I saw that in the garden there were many people working and growing plants and that is what I saw.

One morning I stopped by that garden. I stopped for maybe 10 or 20 minutes. There was one boy who came to me and he said,

"Hi, I'm Wendell."

I said, "Hi, my name is Hina."

Wendell gave me some information about the garden. He said, "I always see you in the that park and you stop here and look at this garden."

He said, "You know what?"

I really liked working in the garden. He said in the garden you can grow flowers, plants, fruits, and vegetables. That time I was really thinking about the vegetables. He asked if I liked the garden and growing plants.

I said, "I have a memory from my country, India, and memory of my friends." And then we talked about the garden. And I asked Wendell about the garden. I asked Wendell if it would be easy for me to grow vegetables. "Can I do this?" Wendell said, "Of course, you can grow vegetables."

"I was very happy."

Wendell said, "I can help you to grow vegetables."

I said "That's great idea." Wendell give me lots of ideas about the garden.

When I started growing vegetables I thought that I had no people to help me for growing vegetables. So I was very worried about this problem. Then my neighbors came to me and asked if they could help me. I said yes. So all my neighbors came and helped me to grow vegetables. And I thought that I had some misunderstanding because I thought they were really rude. They didn't help me for anything. But my neighbors are not like that. So then I was so happy.

Me and my neighbors worked in the garden. Some people put water on the vegetables, some people cut bad plants, some people cleaned the garden.

When I was doing that I felt like I was with my Indian friends working together. So I did not miss them as much. Now I have new friends so that's why I don't miss my Indian friends.

I had some misunderstandings about my neighbors that has gone away. I have some information about the garden. Wendell did help me so much with my garden.

To hear the chapter read by the author, scan the QR code or use the link below.

tinyurl.com/hinaschapter

ESOL 3, Glen Burnie High School, 2015-2016

Image By: Humara

ABOUT GABY

My name is Gaby. I am from Syria. I came to the United States because all my family was here and I liked the United States when I was a little kid. I came to here by airplane because it is very far from my country. I came to live in Glen Burnie because all my family and all the people I know live in Glen Burnie.

When I came to Glen Burnie I didn't like it because it's different than from where I lived back in my country. The first day it was very hard for me because all the people and friends were different and I didn't know anybody and the language was different. It was hard for me because I didn't understand what the people said. After awhile I started to learn some English in school and I started to know some places. I met new friends and we started to play together and do work together in school. We started to go on field trips together. Later I got my license and I bought a car and I started to drive. Then when I got older I found a good job.

I think a person needs time to adapt to new situations in life because when you change your life you will feel like you lost something because it is very hard for everybody when someone moves to a new country. My story it is similar to the *Seedfolks* story because it talked about a garden and all the people in the garden are friends and everybody knows each other. Everybody helps each other in the garden to plant seeds.

My story is similar to Kim's chapter in *Seedfolks* because her family traveled to another country and they helped each other in the garden. They found a good idea to fix the problem when the plants started to die.

GABY'S CHAPTER

My name is Gaby. I am a young man from California. My parents went to another neighborhood because my parents found a new job in Cleveland and all my family and friends lived in this beautiful neighborhood. All of them worked in big garden next to their neighborhood.

It is very big garden all the people help each other. So they told me to come and start working with them.

The same thing happened with my friend Kim who moved from Vietnam to another place and she started to work in the garden and plant a lima beans.

The garden changed our neighborhood because everybody spent all day in the garden and started working because it's the only job for them because they don't have another job in this neighborhood.

We planted a lot stuff in the garden like fruit and vegetables because we needed to get money because we didn't have another job. All the neighbors went to the garden every day to take care of the plants because it was the only thing important for them. So when the plants started to die in the winter we started thinking about what we were going to do to protect the plants. Then we got a good idea and we started to make a greenhouse. We helped each other to protect the plants and keep the plants safe.

The plants are very important to us because we eat from these plants and we sold them to get money because we do not have another job. The good lesson I learned from the garden is not to give up. When the plants started to die in the winter everybody helped each other to make a greenhouse to help the plants to stay alive.

ESOL 3, GLEN BURNIE HIGH SCHOOL, 2015-2016

ABOUT GILDARDO

My name is Gildardo and I'm from Guatemala. I'm 20 years old. I'm a friendly person and I like to make new friends. I lived in Guatemala before I came to Glen Burnie MD. I made the decision to be here because it had been 10 years that I hadn't seen my dad. I felt happy when I saw my dad in the airport and I hugged him.

My first days here were awesome because after 10 years I could share time with my dad and that made me feel good.

I asked him if we could buy some seeds to plant and he told me sure and we went to Home Depot and bought some seeds to plant so we could have a little garden outside of our house I felt excited about that because I spent time with my dad.

The most important thing I liked from the book *Seedfolks*, a book I read in school, was how the community changed when Kim, the main character, started to plant in the garden. After that everybody started to do the same as her.

I related to the book when Kim wanted to share with her dad but the bad thing was the her dad died before she was born. I could spend time with my dad and he is still alive. I was always dreaming when I was in my country to be with my dad and to do things together with him like the garden.

TO HEAR THE CHAPTER READ BY THE AUTHOR, SCAN THE QR CODE OR USE THE LINK BELOW.

tinyurl.com/gabyschapter

ESOL 3, GLEN BURNIE HIGH SCHOOL, 2015-2016

GILDARDO'S CHAPTER

My name is Gildardo and I'm from Guatemala. I came from my country because there was a lot of delinquency. I made the decision to live in Cleveland because I thought it was a good place to live.

But when I came here to Cleveland I saw that this is the worst place to live. I came here because I was looking for a better job and life than I had in my country.

I saw my neighbors from Cleveland as good people but I haven't told them that. When I started to talk to them I could see they are shy people but some of them are rude. Because sometimes I said "Hi" to them but they didn't answer me. One day I was walking from my job and I took a different way home. On my way home I saw a little girl who was planting beans and I started to walk toward her. I asked her if I could come to the garden to plant something that I wanted and she told me, "Sure, you can do that."

I went home to look for some seeds to plant. But I looked for special seeds of bananas because I like them. Then I took them to the garden and I planted them but they didn't grow.

I then made the decision to plant grapes because they are small and grow faster than bananas. I was in the garden with Kim, my neighbor from Cleveland, and we had a traditional conversation. "What is your name? Where are you from?" She told me that she is from Vietnam and I got surprised when she told me that her dad was a farmer. After a week I went to the garden to see how my grapes were growing and I saw they were growing so quickly. That made me feel happy because they thrived quickly and got big too.

Then I saw my neighbors were different than I thought before. When I went to the garden every day I started to talk to them and I started to know some of them because they liked to spend time in the garden. I liked when I saw how the people took care of the garden. They liked to have the garden clean and they watered the plants everyday.

ESOL 3, GLEN BURNIE HIGH SCHOOL, 2015-2016

From that experience I learned that I didn't have to judge people before I knew them. Sometimes you meet new people who are friendly and realize they are not bad people. I got a different experience in the garden because I like to go there and talk to the people. Everyone has different types of ideas.

To hear the chapter read by the author, scan the QR code or use the link below.

tinyurl.com/gildardoschapter

ESOL 3, GLEN BURNIE HIGH SCHOOL, 2015-2016

Image by: Alex

ESOL 3, GLen Burnie HIGH SCHOOL, 2015-2016

ABOUT Humara

My name is Humara. I came from Bangladesh on May 3rd 2013. I came from Bangladesh to America because my grandmother wanted all her siblings to come here and she wanted to come to America too but she died before my birth. Also in America the education is better than in Bangladesh. So many kids come to America to complete a course and sometimes some of them go back to their country to get a good job. If you do a course from United States you can get a good job in Bangladesh. My grandmother knew that there were many more opportunities outside of Bangladesh. That is the reason my grandma made me and my family come to this country.

    I used to live in Odenton when I first came to America. Also my mom and brothers lived here too but my dad wasn't here. My mom and I started working. I started working when I was 14 years old. My uncle found a house in Glen Burnie for my family and my aunt's family. My mom transferred her job to Glen Burnie but I couldn't because where I used to work my aunt was the manager which is why I got the job at 14 years old. No one would give me a job in Glen Burnie and I needed it to help my family. My dad came to the USA after 9 months. I stayed there, went to school and worked for a year and some months. I came to Glen Burnie in the summer of 2014. I stayed home in the summer and didn't do a job. I was waiting until I turned 16 to get a new job because where I used to work when I was 14 was a really a hard job for a kid.

Humara

My name is Humara. I came from Bangladesh on May 3rd 2013. I came to Cleveland Heights because my grandmother wanted all her siblings to come here and she wanted to come to Cleveland Heights too. She died before my birth. My uncle, aunt, my parents and I went to live in Cleveland Heights to make my grandmother's dream come true. Where I live in Cleveland Heights there is no apartment, only houses and they're not far apart. We lived in our uncle's house and not only my parents, brothers and I live there but all my aunt's kids live there too. There are so many kids and so much noise. That made the neighborhood annoying. The neighbors had come to complain so many times for making so much noise. In front of my uncle's house there was so much talking. I saw my uncle was planting beans in the garden and he had other vegetables in the garden too. I was watching it from the window.

Then I went out and I was watching how my uncle was planting beans. I wanted to plant beans in the garden too. Everyone love beans in my family so my uncle said "We can make more beans so we don't have to buy them from the grocery store. I was talking to my uncle and then my aunt came out from the house. They were talking to me about the garden. I said to my uncle and my aunt "how long have you guys have been planting vegetables in the garden?" My aunt said "It's been 3 years that we're planting vegetables in the garden." I said "Why do you guys plant vegetables? You guys can buy them from the grocery store." They both said together "Well the vegetable shop is so far from our house and it's not possible to go there everyday and also we feel great by planting and taking care of them." So I planted beans in the garden and I watered my plants everyday in the evening. The summer beans grew up fast and nicely in this season. Our plants look so pretty because everything is green and all the vegetables grow nicely. There are so many tomatoes, beans, chili peppers and other vegetable plants that my uncle brought from my country. I don't know all of their names. My neighbors exercise in the evening in the summer. Most of them look at our garden and wonder what we are making in the garden. They stand outside of our garden and watch how we plant vegetables in the garden.

My aunt goes for a walk in the evening in the summer. She saw an old man start to plant tomatoes in his yard. She came to our house and tells us that she saw this. The next day when she went for a walk again she saw he planted beans too. That old man maybe liked how we planted vegetables in our yard and that's why he started to plant. We didn't know we inspired others to plant vegetables too.

The old man's house behind our house looked good when everything was green and red. The garden looked so beautiful. Other neighbors started to plant in their yards by seeing us and the old man. They didn't plant because their family loved beans. They planted them because they thought it would make the community look pretty and they all have fun by working together. Also everyone gets to meet each other every evening. I learned that when people do something or make something they don't do it on purpose. They don't think that other people will love to do it too but it makes changes. For example, we never knew our neighbors would plant vegetables in their yard by seeing us. I felt so good by seeing everyone working together.

To hear the chapter read by the author, scan the QR code or use the link below.

tinyurl.com/humaraschapter

ESOL 3, GLEN BURNIE HIGH SCHOOL, 2015-2016

IMAGE BY: TEMA ENCARNACION

ABOUT NABIL

My name is Nabil. I am from Bangladesh. I came to the United States because me and family didn't feel safe in Bangladesh. Then my dad contacted my uncle who was the one who sponsored us to come here and he said we will be safe here. So we moved to the USA in 2013. After we came here for the first 3 month we lived in Crofton, MD because my uncle's house was there. Then my dad found a better job in Glen Burnie. So we moved to Glen Burnie and started living here from then on.

My first day in the United States was confusing because in my free time I play soccer or play cricket with my cousins but none of my cousin lives in here so I had to play video games in my free time.

In my ESOL class I read a book called *Seedfolks*. It was about farming. In that book a character called Gonzalo had to make all his dad's phone calls because his dad didn't speak English. This chapter relates to my story because I make my dad's phone calls as well because my dad doesn't speak English.

One thing that impacted me from *Seedfolks* is when Kim's sister and mother were crying front of her father's photo. Then she took a spoon from the kitchen and some lima beans and walked outside to plant beans in memory of her father. She never saw her father but she knew her father liked gardening. So she plants some beans in the vacant lot in her neighborhood. She had no such memory of her father but she thinks her father will see her planting beans for him but he will not recognize who she is. She believed she could plant like her father because she is his daughter.

Another thing that impacted me from *Seedfolks* was that when Leona walked down the street she felt a bad smell from the garbage bag. She told people to clean it up. But no one wanted to clean it up. So she called the health department to clean it up. But they didn't take her seriously. The next morning she took a garbage bag to the health department to show them how bad it smells. The employee there smells the garbage bag and told her to leave and the next day they will send someone to clean it up. That impacted me because she was the only one who took the responsibility to clean up the mess.

Nabil's Chapter

My name is Nabil. I am from Bangladesh. I came to United States to get a better education so I would be able to get a better job because the level of education is way better here than in my country. My view of the neighborhood is that it looks beautiful when you look up to the sky, but it's kind of dirty when you look down in the parking lot. Sometimes people play loud music which causes problems.

One day I was walking down the street and I saw a garden. There was a tree where I planned to plant some beans. There were some people who were walking around that garden and I asked them if anyone could plant there and they said yes. Even they planted there too. They were planting in the garden because their parents liked to have a garden. Then I planted some beans because I wanted to have my own plants too and I put some water on them. But I didn't put water on them regularly so the plants started dying. But when I put water on the plants everyday for a week then they started to grow again. After 1 or 2 months they died, though. I don't know why but they died.

People in my neighborhood started making their own garden in their yard. My view of my neighborhood changed a lot and now it looks even nicer than it did before. One thing I learned from this experience is that nothing is impossible if you have the mindset to do it.

To hear the chapter read by the author, scan the QR code or use the link below.

tinyurl.com/nabilschapter

ESOL 3, GLEN BURNIE HIGH SCHOOL, 2015-2016

IMAGE BY: TEMA ENCARNACION

ESOL 3, GLEN BURNIE HIGH SCHOOL, 2015-2016

ABOUT PEDRO

My name is Pedro. I was born in Mexico but I came to the United States when I was 8 months old and now I am 14. I basically lived here my whole life. First when I came here to the United States I had to cross the border. It's a difficult obstacle to cross. First I went into Texas and stayed there for one day. My uncles that lived here in Glen Burnie came to pick me and my parents up from Texas.

I came to the United States so me and my family could have a better life. When we came here to the United States we lived with my uncle. My parents found a job and then when me and my family were all settled we got our own home. Then when I was 3 my baby brother was born. At age 4 is when I started going school. In pre-k I was scared since I was on my own and my parents weren't with me to help me. I thought everyone there was going to be mean but I got to meet everyone and they were all nice and the students helped me out if I needed help. Everyone there became good friends. Now I'm in high school. I came far from pre-k to highschool. Right now I'm in the 9th grade.

This can relate to the book *Seedfolks* because people from the book came from other countries to have a better life. Something that *Seedfolks* taught me was that family doesn't mean you have to be family by blood but because you have each other whenever and love each other.

TO HEAR THE CHAPTER READ BY THE AUTHOR, SCAN THE QR CODE OR USE THE LINK BELOW.

tinyurl.com/pedroschapter

Pedro's Chapter

It's been two years that I have been living in Cleveland Heights, Ohio. I came to Cleveland to have a better life since in my country we needed a life we would like so we moved to Ohio.

It was a hard process coming to live here. We had to cross the border and it was something really difficult for us. My family has been trying to get to the United States for a long time. We were outside for some days and had to hide and go over the border. It was a really hard process to do.

The neighborhood I'm living in now is not the best or fanciest. A lot of immigrants come live here for a better life. We have problems here in this neighborhood. People always leave trash everywhere and they don't clean it up. One day I was walking and I came across this garden one mile away from my house. Each day I always go to the garden to plant and garden because it's something I love doing. In the garden I plant watermelons because they're something I love eating and it reminds me of my father because he used to plant watermelons in Mexico. In the garden there is this old man who is always in the garden. Me and him became good friends. He always talks to me about his family and we talk about the garden.

The watermelons take a long time to grow. It takes about a month and just 2 weeks to start thriving. My neighborhood is not a nice neighborhood and my view of the people is that they're all bad people. One day this guy was going to run over my garden and this man came out of his house and made the guy leave and didn't run over my garden. And this made me change my point of view about my neighborhood. A lesson I have learned is that it is not good to judge people by how they look if you don't know them.

ESOL 3, Glen Burnie High School, 2015-2016

ABOUT ROHA

My name is Roha and I am a Pakistani. I am 14 and I am in ninth grade. I came to the United States when I was 12. When we came here my father got a job and we moved to Glen Burnie. It was summer vacation and my father and brother would go to their jobs regularly. After the summer vacation was over and we got admission into school, my older brother and sister went to high school and I went to middle school. At that time I was really nervous because I didn't speak any English but people were nice so I survived middle school.

Now, in my high school ESOL 3 class we read *Seedfolks* where a garden brings the whole community together. There was a chapter which reminded me of something like my friends and teachers. In Amir's chapter Amir's name reminded me of a teacher in Pakistan named

Amir and this reminded me of my school in Pakistan. The thing that impacted me the most in *Seedfolks* was Leona's chapter when she talked about keeping our environment clean. This impacted me because in reality people don't do that. When we were reading *Seedfolks* we learned about Flint, Michigan and nobody tried anything to clean the rivers or the pipes. I think if there is a clean environment nothing bad would happen and the community will feel the improvement too.

To hear the chapter read by the author, scan the QR code or use the link below.

tinyurl.com/rohaschapter

ESOL 3, GLEN BURNIE HIGH SCHOOL, 2015-2016

ROHA'S CHAPTER

When l left Pakistan I was really cheerless because I would miss my dad's side's loyal cousins and my fantastic friends. I came to the United States because my aunt wanted us to come to the USA. Life at first wasn't hard but then school started and I was sick. I threw up so many times because I was so nervous. I was so scared about meeting new people. In middle school sometimes I used to not understand what other people would say.

Now after two years life is easier because I understand what my teachers and others say. Cleveland is not famous and it's like no one knows it even exists. I didn't understand why we couldn't live with our aunt in Bowie. It's so stinky in Cleveland that there are dead rats everywhere. But what can I do? My dad's job is here. I'm always scared to go outside because I don't even know if someone is going to get murdered or beat up by a thief.

One time I was coming home from the grocery store with my awkward sister and sweet mom and you wouldn't believe what I saw. I knew I saw something magical like an impossible dream, but it was really a fascinating garden. I went home quickly and I asked my mom for money to buy seeds. She refused. Then I insisted and she gave me money. Me and my sister went to an old seed shop excitedly. We got rose seeds and we both came back to the vacant lot and eventually after trying so hard we found a place. We both started digging. While planting I was missing my cousins but I controlled myself and my friends and that was the reason I planted the roses like my uncle's rose garden.

After that I saw a girl. She was similar in age to me, or maybe older, but she was pregnant at such a young age. She said, "there was a boy who cheated on me." I didn't want to make her bitter so I changed the topic quickly and asked her, "Why are you planting radishes?" She said "There is a class for pregnant teenage girls and together we are planting radishes because they are easy and grow well." It was getting late so we went back to our home. They started to grow incredibly well. After some days the roses started thriving. Their smell was excellent. People from the garden came and were asking me for roses. The pregnant girl was really happy and joyful because our glamorous roses were near her boring radishes. One time the pregnant girl told me about the Puerto Rican boy who was coming to their side and was trying to talk to her friend. It was obvious that she was jealous.

One day I came calmly to the garden to water my beautiful roses. Nobody was in the garden yet. It's because it was early morning and everyone was sleeping. When I went to the garden and I saw my rose bush and I was shocked because my roses were missing. I was really heartbroken. Then I was thinking about what the pregnant girl told me to do if I wanted to keep my roses safe. I have to put something around them. There I saw a boy and it was none other than the garden guard Royce. I went furiously to him and asked him about my rose. Royce was looking panicked. I asked him again. He said "I don't know! You didn't give me anything to take care of your plants." He was so rude but then he finally agreed to take care of my roses. It was a joy.

The whole community was changed because of the garden. I wasn't scared to go out anymore. There was something that I learned from this garden and the people in it. That we just need to take one step and we can change the world, we just need to try harder and not give up. There was someone who started this garden and then by looking at it other people started doing it and they didn't stop even if the weather was bad and they kept trying.

ESOL 3, GLEN BURNIE HIGH SCHOOL, 2015-2016

IMAGE BY: Tema Encarnacion

ABOUT SAMIP

I am a normal high school student who loves to live an easy life. My name is Samip. I came from Nepal. The reason I came to the United States was because my family thought studying abroad would help me get a better education than anywhere else. I came to live in Glen Burnie because my family was here. I was really excited to come to Glen Burnie. I remember my first day in Glen Burnie. My father took me out to show me around. I was really surprised to see how different it was from my country. When I walked out in the streets it made me feel so odd because everyone was speaking a different language. I felt really uneasy but I got used to it in about a month.

After I joined high school, in my ESOL 3 class we read a book called *Seedfolks*. The book is about different people from different places who were trying to make their society clean and plant a lot of trees. In this book there's a chapter called Amir. In the chapter the guy named Amir said that when he first came to the United States, he felt that "everyone is a foe, unless they are known to be friends." Something like that was going on with me as well. I was afraid to talk to others unless I knew they were friendly.

Seedfolks is a great book. It really impacted me. When I read that people were working together to build up their city, I learned that when people work together to do something it is meant to be completed.

Samip's Chapter

I grew up in a neighborhood where there were a lot of trees and plants. My name is Samip. Now I am here in the United States. I came from Nepal. The reason I came here was because my mother and father were here. The neighborhood that I moved to wasn't as good as the one from my country. The neighborhood in Cleveland was not clean. It was full of garbage. There was not even a single tree out in the streets. It was like nobody knew how to plant anything. None of the people were cooperative with each other. Everyone stayed at home and did their own thing. One day when I was walking down the street carrying my groceries, I saw some people working in a lot surrounded by three walls. Later, I found out that it was a garden. I was so happy to find out that there were still some people who liked to plant a vegetable garden. I asked them if I could plant something in the garden. They said I could.

The next day I came back with some carrot seeds. I chose carrots because I liked eating them. When I was planting, I came across a guy named Sam. I was so curious about what he was planting so I asked him, "Hey Sam, what are you planting?" With a big smile he said, "I am planting pumpkins because I could get a lot of money by selling pumpkins during Halloween." After that I told him that I planted carrots because they are my favourite. We talked a lot that day. I was really happy to make a new friend. I took care of my carrots everyday and I watered them daily. My carrots grew really big. I didn't have any problem growing them. I think that was the result of my hard work.

I was happy that my carrots grew well but there was still something that was bothering me. The uneasiness that I had with the people in my neighborhood. I was so upset that only some of the people were working. But later on they came together. The thing that brought them together must have been all those vegetables in the garden. Different people planted different vegetables. They were so nicely grown everyone must have wanted them. They thought that working together might help them to get everything they wanted so they worked together. I think seeing us working also made the people in the neighborhood realize that this might be the way to make our neighborhood clean and healthy. One after another started coming. They helped each other.

The happiness of doing work with many people is much greater than the happiness you get from doing it alone. I also learned that unity is everything. It gives you the strength to do the work you can't do alone. I learned this when I saw two guys working together. I was working alone in the garden as always. A guy came out of nowhere and started digging a hole. He was so bad that he couldn't even dig a hole properly. I just looked at him and did nothing. After a minute later another guy came and asked him if he needed help. Then the second guy helped the poor guy to dig a hole and plant his seeds. When I saw that I realized that this happens when you work together. Everything went fine afterward.

To hear the chapter read by the author, scan the QR code or use the link below.

tinyurl.com/samipschapter

ESOL 3, GLEN BURNIE HIGH SCHOOL, 2015-2016

IMAGE BY: KELLY REIDER

ABOUT SHAHIN

My name is Shahin. I am 20 years old. I am from India. I came to the U.S.A because my father's whole family is here. I have a big and nice family. I like my friends from my country. When my dream of coming to the U.S.A. finally came true, I was so happy. But when the day finally arrived I was so sad and I was crying with my family and friends.

On February 21, 2014 I came in the U.S.A. Thirteen people in my family came together at the same time. My uncle, aunt and all her children came together. When I came to the U.S.A. I didn't sleep because it was hard for me because the time in my country and here is totally different. On my first day here I was so happy because all my family was waiting to meet us. I was so excited to meet them.

I like it here but I still miss my country. Some places are beautiful here. But when I have school breaks I want to go to my country for vacation. My first day in Glen Burnie High school was nice but not very good because I didn't speak perfect English. When I came to the United States I was so sad because we did not have a job or car or any idea what we could do and how could we make the money. Then we tried to apply for jobs and also my father's family helped us. Then finally we had good job, a car and everything.

When I came here I was sad because I left my friends and family and also because I didn't know the English language very well. Then I went to school and got a job. I learned lots of new things in my life with teachers and my new friends in United States.

In a *Seedfolks*, Curtis' chapter talked about growing tomatoes. Curtis grew the tomatoes to impress his girlfriend. I like to grow tomatoes also because we can use them in our cooking. When I wrote about *Seedfolk* I felt nice because I learned lots of new and important things in my life. I like this book it was nice story.

SHAHIN'S CHAPTER

In India we have lots of good places. When I was 9 years old, I was going to school. I had a lot of friends in school. I was so excited to go to school everyday because it was so fun with friends to talk with in the classes. I was born in India. I like my village better than the city. In the village we had a nice neighborhood. I loved my family. I had a big and good family. In India and in the U.S.A. too.

When my grandfather sponsored us, after 12 years we came to the U.S.A. When I came to the U.S. A. I was so happy. I didn't know how I could show my happiness. Then finally that day came and when it came I was so sad and I cried with all my friends and neighbors because I was sad to leave them. When I was in the airport I couldn't believe myself. I was like, "I am in the U.S.A." I had to question myself.

I was finally in the U.S.A. My family was almost here. We lived together in my aunt's house. Then we moved to Cleveland Heights, because my father had work here and me and my brother had good opportunities to study here. So, that's why we moved here. Then I was going to college and I made many good friends. But, I still missed my friends in my country.

But in the U.S.A. life is so busy. When I was in school I was busy in classes. When I was at work, I was busy with working and when I was at home I was busy helping my mother make food, cleaning the house etc. So, I didn't have time to talk with my old friends.

When the guests come to the house and they make lots of noise that was a problem sometimes. It is okay but when I was reading or doing homework it disturbed me. I went outside with my grandfather and walked. Everyday I did something. One day, I walked and I asked my grandfather, "Can we go to this side?" My grandfather said "Okay". That day, I saw a beautiful garden with flowers.

Then we went in the garden and we met the people that were planting and watering in the garden. We got information about the garden. Then I came home and I talked with my parents about the garden. One day, I was sitting and I was thinking about the garden. Then I decided I will also plant something in my garden. Finally, I decided I will grow tomatoes because they will help to make food. I can make more money also and I can share with my good neighbors.

I was again in that garden and that time I met Nora. I was asking her about the garden and for information about planting tomatoes. I watered my plants everyday. I took care of my plants in the garden. When the weather was good I went outside in my garden and listened to the music too.

One day, my neighbors' children were playing in my garden and they broke my plants. I was so sad. I felt like they broke my heart because everyday I took care of my plants so I missed them. When I missed my plants my neighbors didn't see my happiness and they changed their mind. They decided now they will grow the plants that got ruined and they would make me happy again like before. I love my neighborhoods. We enjoyed the garden again.

The lesson I learned from planting in the garden was if we love each other and help each other then nobody can break our love. Always we must share with people and help them. If you share with them then also one day they will do the same thing with you. If you have an idea it is important to tell other people and explain to them. It makes you so proud of yourself.

TO HEAR THE CHAPTER READ BY THE AUTHOR, SCAN THE QR CODE OR USE THE LINK BELOW.

tinyurl.com/shahinschapter

ESOL 3, GLEN BURNIE HIGH SCHOOL, 2015-2016

Image by: Tema Encarnacion

ESOL 3, GLEN BURNIE HIGH SCHOOL, 2015-2016

ABOUT AYOMIDE

My name is Ayomide, I am 13 years old. I am from Nigeria and I moved to America because my father lived here and he wanted me to come to live in America. I came here 4 years ago, I moved 3 times in America. First I moved to Laurel from Lanham, and to Glen Burnie from Laurel.

The first day I moved to Glen Burnie, my neighborhood was really quiet but if the kids came out to play it was kind of loud.

I can relate my story of coming to Glen Burnie to Nora, a nurse in the book called *Seedfolks*. The book talks about a garden that brought people together. Nora takes care of a man called Mr. Myles who reminds me of my grandfather who was also in a wheelchair. That also encourages me. I used to take care of him. It makes my happy because Nora takes care of Mr. Myles and he is still alive. When I see Nora taking Mr. Myles for a walk I am encouraged because if she can then I can.

What impacted me the most in the book was when people in the city were not talking to each other but only people of their own race. That made me feel sad because it is good to be friends with each other.

TO HEAR THE CHAPTER READ BY THE AUTHOR, SCAN THE QR CODE OR USE THE LINK BELOW.

tinyurl.com/ayomidechapter

AYOMIDE'S CHAPTER

I came from Nigeria. I moved from my country to America because my father was here. When I moved, I was so different from other kids because I acted weird, and I had an accent. When I was taking a walk to get to know the neighborhood better, I noticed something about it. It was so dirty, bad, and messy.

While I was walking, a Puerto Rican kid came up to me. I thought he wanted to be nice and say hi to me, but instead he wanted me to buy some weed from him. I gave him a stink eye, and walked away.

While I was walking I also came across a beautiful garden. Everyone in the garden looked so happy. I wanted to plant something beautiful in the garden, so I decided to plant sunflowers because they grow up to be beautiful.

I also came across Nora. Nora is my caring neighbor. She takes care of Mr. Myles. Mr. Myles is a friend of my dad. I asked how he was doing, and she said "He is doing good but he misses his mother so much." Mr.Myles' mother died with cancer. Mr. Myles planted hollyhocks, poppies, and snapdragons to remember his mother.

I went for a walk about week later, and the sunflower that I planted didn't even think about growing. I was so mad. While I was getting over my disappointment, I saw a man, I guessed his name was Sam because everybody talked about him. He was trying to get people to talk to each other, I think the garden brought people together, and that's a good thing. Some people didn't even want to communicate with each other, especially if they were a different race, and that's not a good thing.

I figured that if an old man can try to bring people together, why can't I try too.

ABOUT Trang

My name is Trang. I'm 19 year old and I am friendly. Some people see me and say I'm not friendly because I am quiet. It's so hard when people talk with me, because when I'm talking with people I don't say very much. Sometimes, I'm confused when people want to talk with me because I really want to speak with them.

I'm from Vietnam and I went to the United States, and I live in Glen Burnie because my grandmother lives right here. She lived here for about 27 years. I have lived here about two and a half years. My parents told me that when I come to the USA I should live in Glen Burnie because I can study and get a good education. My dream of coming to the U.S. is to take care of my grandmother because she is old and she needs me to take care of her when she is sick.

When I arrived the first day in the USA I was so surprised about how big everything is. I have a problem, though, which is the language. My language in my country is different than here and that was difficult for me. I worried about that because if I don't understand the language here. I couldn't talk or come to school. So I tried to study English and to talk a little bit with my grandma. However my grandma is not good about talking but it helped when I came to live here.

I'm reading *Seedfolks* in my ESOL class. This is a story similar to my life and Kim's life. The main character's father died and I have my brother who also died . That was so sad and I can feel that from her story when I read the first or chapter of *Seedfolks*. I remembered my brother and it hurt and wanted to cry but I couldn't because I was in school and I knew I shouldn't cry. I never gave up when I was reading Seedfolks in class. I understand I must change my life and I learned more from this book.

Trang's Chapter

My father was from China. He is a serious man. My mother was from Vietnam. She is a smart woman and she has a job. My father met my mother when my mother had a job in the company of my father. They met and fell more in love day by day. After that they were married and I was born and then my brother. I was happy and had perfect parents. But one day, my brother was hanging out with his classmates in school and was unlucky. He had an accident. When my family and me knew that we were shocked and couldn't believe that. I couldn't control myself, my mom and dad were so sad, their hearts were broken and mine too.

We went quickly to the accident. "Oh my God." I just said. My dream about family has a mom, dad and brother. I couldn't imagine the dream. My parents cried too much because they lost their son and I lost my brother. After he died, I didn't go anywhere, I just stayed in my room and cried. I was thinking if I cried I couldn't solve the problem that is occurring, so I must be calm. I went out and walk around to relax my mind. When I walking my friend saw me and called me. "That was long ago," he told with me. He knew what happened with my family and me. He was sad too, because his sister and my brother were in love. His sister cried too much. Of course, I knew my brother's death made everybody sad. We went to my home and talked. He shared with me a lot of things, so I could reduce my sorrow.

"You shouldn't sit here or cry or anything about your problems. It's not good for you, you can get sick".

I know that. For three days I couldn't eat anything. He put food in my mouth, I just ate a little.

"Don't think negatively, you must think about the positive, you have many things you haven't done so try to do more".

He was right and I knew that, now I changed my life. I went to America, because I knew that. I could learn something new about culture there and a achieve my real dream of becoming a pharmacist. I take care of my parents that my grandmother is here. I have met and become acquainted with my neighbor. He is very tall and handsome, he was from Korea. I like him. He is very friendly. He looks like my brother but he is different. My brother was serious and quiet but he is so energetic and talked too much. Sometimes we fought because he was so crazy but he was fun.

I walked outside to the garden at his house. The garden is so beautiful. My cousin was a farmer of flowers such as roses, sunflowers, lavenders. I helped him take care of the flowers and he taught me how he plants rainbow roses, black roses, he planted it in a separate place. Because it was special.

So, I asked him, "Do you know a flower named mimosa?" He knew it. That flower is from Japan and the color of the flower is so beautiful and is pink and yellow. "Do you know how you can plant it?" I asked my cousin. He told me that he didn't know, so I had to search in books for more information about mimosas. When I found that I quickly bought the plant. I went to plant them because my brother gave me a gift of that flower when he came back home from work and he always gave me pink mimosas.

I told Kim about my garden, because she was from Vietnam and speaks my same language, so we understand each other. We are girls so we feel the same. She asked me." Why do you plant mimosas and not another flower?" I explained to her and she was surprised about my reason. She planted lima beans because she remembers her father from Vietnam. I planted in my yard. I followed the instructions step by step on the back of the flower packet. Now it is growing and thriving and the mimosa flowers on the tree are so beautiful.

One day, I came home from my neighborhood and I saw a garden and there was a bad smell of trash. I shared something new, ideas from my for garden. You could plant some flowers or trees here and they could smell good. She liked it too and we had fun planting the garden and learning more about taking care of the garden. I changed my life

ESOL 3, GLEN BURNIE HIGH SCHOOL, 2015-2016

and I never give up when I have any difficulties. I will try to pass this on as it helps me to learn more and have more experiences in my life. I can find the path I choose thanks to myself and some friends who encouraged me when I have bad problems or difficulties.

To hear the chapter read by the author, scan the QR code or use the link below.

tinyurl.com/trangschapter

ESOL 3, GLEN BURNIE HIGH SCHOOL, 2015-2016

ABOUT TRUC

I am Truc. I am from Vietnam and I came here because my grandmother stayed here to get a great life and then she wanted to pick up my family to live with her. So I came with my family and we live in Glen Burnie, Maryland.

On my first day in Glen Burnie, it was so boring because everything had changed. I did not go to school at that time I stayed home for the first 3 months and didn't do anything. I just lived alone, nobody stayed with me except my grandma because everyone had a job and they needed to work. It made me frustrated at myself and I wanted to go back to my country. I cried every night and I asked my mom to let me go back to my country. I didn't want to live in the U.S because I missed my family and my friends in Vietnam.

I did not know English when I came here. My speaking and listening were not good so I couldn't communicate with anyone. I was so sad, and my mom asked me " Do you want go to school?" I was very scared because I was not good at English. I wondered how can I come to school to study and get new friends. But my mom told me not to be scared because I am grown so I need to be strong. So I tried and I went to school and the first day I took the bus without my parents in a new country. I thought it would be hard to study but it was not. When I came to school my new teacher was so nice. She's very friendly and funny. She taught an ESOL newcomer class so I had a lot of things to study in this class.

My story relates with the chapter of Sea Young in *Seedfolks*. *Seedfolks* is a book that I read in my ESOL class and is about someone who has a new life and they were the first new family in a new place. They needed to find the new thing and study, they are like seeds when you plant them and they grow. I had to read this book in my ESOL class and I saw Sea Young's chapter. She is a person in a new country and she doesn't know anything. Then her husband died and she was

ESOL 3, Glen Burnie High School, 2015-2016

left alone. When she worked in her shop she had an accident. She was attacked by an armed robber. So she was scared to go outside. She just lived in her house and only opened her door to collect the food her neighbors bought her and she hired someone to watch her shop. After a long time she went outside. This shows about how at first she did not know anything and she had some trouble so she felt bad but she did not give up. She is like me when I first came here. I was scared of everything and I felt upset but I never gave up. I persevered when things were hard.

    The book is about the life of someone who had to move in a new country. It's a hard time to do your work but you need to be strong to overcome it and get a good life. In my chapter I want to tell everyone if you have to change your life in a new country you need to be strong because if you are not strong you can not get a great life. If you're strong you cannot give up.

To hear the chapter read by the author, scan the QR code or use the link below.

tinyurl.com/trucschapter

Truc's Chapter

My family lived in Vietnam. It was beautiful, large, nice place but my aunt in my country wanted to get a great life so she moved to the United States. She brought my family to live with her. After a few years my family moved to Cleveland Heights, so everything was again new. I had a new house, new school, new friends and a especially I had a new neighborhood. My new neighbors were so nice and they are not noisy like in my country. But I have a little problem with them, I did not know why they kept looking at me all the time and watching what was I doing.

One day when I went to school on my bus, I looked out of a window to see. Everything here is so peaceful and beautiful and I saw a garden. It's not far from my house and nobody planted in it so my family bought it to plant some vegetables like basil and cilantro. Because in my country we always planted a garden. So I wanted to plant it and remember where I was born and raised. It also reminds me of so many memories in my country.

After a few weeks my plant grew so fast and I saw my neighbor keep coming near me. They asked me why I planted vegetables in the garden. I told them, "Because it reminded me of my country." My plants are growing so fast in my garden. They have beautiful green leaves.

One day I was in the dirt and my neighbors kept looking at me. They thought I hid something in the dirt so they took out the binoculars to see what I was doing and they knew I planted some more vegetables in the garden. So they knew I'm not hiding something bad so they stopped looking at me everyday.

After I moved in a new house I learned about something new. I can know how to make friends with everyone and I can know how to plant vegetables.

ESOL 3, GLEN BURNIE HIGH SCHOOL, 2015-2016

IMAGE BY: TRANG

ABOUT UTSAB

I am an Asian boy. Everyone called me Nepali but my name is Utsab. I moved from Nepal on November 05, 2014. In my country there was a natural disaster which damaged houses and for that reason I came to the US. When I came to the US, my father worked at an airport as a taxi driver. My sister studied nursing at Baltimore Washington Hospital in Glen Burnie and so we started to live in Glen Burnie.

On the first day when I came to Glen Burnie, I went to parks behind my house. Then I met many friends and we played. They were very friendly. While returning home I saw some Indian people next to my door. The next day, they called me to their house. We are friends from the first day to until today.

In my ESOL 3 class at Glen Burnie High School, we read *Seedfolks*. A book where all the people are migrants from different places. This book is about the community garden where people plant different plants in a community that had a lot of crime in it. All of the chapters are good and interesting to read. I liked Amir's chapter. Amir was from India, I am form Nepal which is a neighbor of India. He sees all the beautiful colors of the garden among the dark brick of the apartment building. I live in an apartment. He loves colors in fabrics but he thinks that the colors in the garden are not for your eyes to see but "to make your eyes see your neighbors" I think people can communicate with each other by the garden by planting. Amir notices how the garden brings the people together for more than just the garden. In the apartment some people did the wrong thing then other people think that the community is bad. Amir realizes he has never met different people from different countries until he came to the garden. I didn't see other people until I left my country.

Utsab's Chapter

ESOL 3, Glen Burnie High School, 2015-2016

When I was a happy child, I always liked being with my honest friends because I played with my friends and travelled to different places in my city. Then I left beautiful Nepal with my family to come to America for a better education and a job for my father. My father's job was a cab driver. He wanted to do this in America because there are no safety rules in Nepal and it is dangerous. When I came here, I was afraid of American people and how they act.

One day when I came travelling from the grocery store I saw a wonderful garden. There was a virtuous girl who was planting beautiful plants. I thought that I could plant cauliflower to honor my grandfather who died after I was born. I planted cauliflower because it reminded me of my grandfather who always planted and he always took care of the cauliflower.

Cauliflower is the favourite vegetable of my grandfather. The next day I went in the gorgeous garden to plant cauliflower. There I met an honorable girl. We both introduced ourselves. Her name was Kim. I asked her, "Why are you planting seeds?" She answered, "I planted seeds for the memory of my father." I said, "I want to honor my grandfather with cauliflower."

We planted together. All the plants were growing well. All the community people came to support and to be friendly with us. All the people have changed their habits from smoking cigarettes to other, better things.

After some days there was a heavy snow. It killed the beautiful plants. I was sad the plants died. I cried a lot remembering the plants for my grandfather.

To hear the chapter read by the author, scan the QR code or use the link below.

tinyurl.com/utsabschapter

ABOUT ZOIYA

My name is Zoiya. I am 16 years old. I am a Muslim and I am from Pakistan. I am friendly with everyone. Me, my parents and my two siblings all live together.

I came to the USA on April 19th, 2014. I came to the US because my aunt sponsored us and it was one of my dreams to come to the US. The first day I came here it was hard for me to adjust at first because of the time change. When it was morning here, it was night in Pakistan so it disturbed my sleep pattern. Also the taste of food was different, and it was hard for me to adjust.

It was so hard for me when I went to school for the first time because I didn't know a lot of English and I saw everyone and I was used to sitting alone on one side. But then I made some friends and they were from my country.

Seedfolks is a book that I read in my ESOL 3 class. In *Seedfolks* it talks about how a garden made the whole community stay together, clean their place and stopped fighting. We read *Seedfolks* because it had some stuff for us to learn like growing plants, staying together, cleaning up and to stop fighting.

I felt sad because Kim lost her father and someone lost their plants. But I learned something from *Seedfolks*, that you shouldn't just think about yourself but how things are affecting your community.

ESOL 3, GLEN BURNIE HIGH SCHOOL, 2015-2016

Zoiya's Chapter

Me and my family moved from Pakistan to the U.S. I came to America at the age of 13 years old. My aunt sponsored me and my family when I was 6 years old. I stayed with my aunt for 3 months and then we moved to Cleveland Heights because my dad had work in Cleveland. When we moved to Cleveland there were a lot of people moving from Cleveland Heights.

People were moving from there because there were a lot of work problems and I heard people fight a lot. I was scared of leaving my apartment. I was scared because I thought if I went outside and someone's fighting maybe they will come to me and start fighting with me so I was afraid.

There were buildings next to my apartment and we had a park in the apartment complex. The problem was that no one went to the park or tried to communicate with each other. I was on my way to school one day and I saw a beautiful garden with a lot of flowers, fruits, and vegetables.

In the garden I saw a woman named Leona. I said, "Hey, how are you?" Leona responded, "I am good, how about you?" I said, "Good, I heard that there was a trash problem in the lot where the garden is right now. I asked, "Who solved the problem and how?" Leona said, "I solved that problem. I called the health department and as usual they put me on hold. But then I took the trash bag filled with trash and went to the health department. I opened the trash bag to make them realize how we live in that smell and how people get sick because of it. I asked, "Did they help you?" Leona, "Yes they did help me." I said, "I need to go. Bye." Leona said, "Bye."

I grew pumpkins in the garden because my grandfather loved pumpkins. So I grew pumpkins as a memory of my grandfather. I took care of my plants. I watered my plants everyday. But one day a lot of ants went on my plants and ruined them. I was feeling cheerless because I did a lot of hard work to grow the plants.

ESOL 3, Glen Burnie High School, 2015-2016

When I grew plants there were a lot of people who came out of their houses to see me and the other people planting together and they started planting too. When the other people started planting and coming out of their houses in a lot of ways they started communicating with each other. This made me feel happy because everyone was together and everyone was talking to each other.

After everyone started communicating with each other they took care of the plants and the garden. Everyone started growing plants, vegetables, and flowers. People stopped throwing trash from their windows to the lot. They kept the lot clean so it wouldn't affect the plants and the people in community. I felt happy because of mine and other people's plants. Everyone got together and talked to each other. No one fights anymore and no one cares if someone is black, white, or Asian.

I learned how a garden could make the whole community come together and stay with each other.

To hear the chapter read by the author, scan the QR code or use the link below.

tinyurl.com/zoiyaschapter

ESOL 3, GLEN BURNIE HIGH SCHOOL, 2015-2016

Image by: Samip

About Cesar

I'm Cesar. I'm from Mexico and I'm 15 years old. I came here about 2 years ago because in Mexico there is too much delinquency and also because we wanted to see my mother's family because I didn't know them. I came here to know them. I came to live to Glen Burnie because all my uncles and aunts live here so my whole family and I got an apartment. When I was in Mexico I never imagined that I could come to the U.S. I didn't learn any English in Mexico so when I first came here it was difficult because I didn't know any English. It was hard to learn English.

In my ESOL class we read a book called *Seedfolks*. It was very interesting. One thing that happened in the book that I could relate with it in the book there is an old man called Sam that wants to be everyone's friend. I also try to be everyone's friend. In the book all the people from different races are separated just because some of them don't like the other people just because they are all different. Sam doesn't like that so he tries to get everyone close so they can talk to each other. I also don't like that. One thing from the book that impacted me was that just because the little girl came out and planted some things everyone wanted to do that for a special reason.

ESOL 3, GLEN BURNIE HIGH SCHOOL, 2015-2016

Cesar's Chapter

    Mexico is very dangerous because there are too many dangerous people and places. That's why we moved to Cleveland. It was awful and there was a lot of trash every where and it didn't smell as good as other places. There were too many homeless people. At night there were a lot of gangs. This place is not safe for us.

    One day when we were walking down the street to go to the grocery store to buy some food for, we saw this girl hiding behind a refrigerator looking at some bean plants and looking sad. Then I came close to her and said "Why are you mad?" And she told me " Because it's kind of an altar for my father that died before I was born. I'm sad because I didn't have any memories from my father and I'm planting this because my father was a farmer in Vietnam. I'm doing this in his honor." I get sad really quickly because of what the little Asian girl told me. Then the next day when I was walking down the street because we were going to the grocery store again and also because the day was boring. When we were really far away from the apartment an old man with gray hair came close to us and start talking to me. He told me " Hi my name is Sam and I hear that you are the new people that just moved to this area. Is that true?" And I said "Yes we are the new people is this area Sam" and Sam said "And what do you think about the neighborhood" and I told him "I think the neighborhood is awful I don't like it because it is too dangerous and there are too many gangs and homeless people and also there is a lot of trash around it so I don't like the neighborhood" and he said "You are gonna change the way you think of the neighborhood. You will see. Well gotta go see you later and good luck here" I responded " Ok see you and thanks."

    Then the next day I saw this little girl again in the garden. In that moment I thought of planting some plants to help the garden look better and the garden can get more flowers. I thought of planting some potatoes in the garden. Every day each week after I came from work I went to the garden to plant the potatoes. I put a fence around the plants because the other day I saw someone getting a tomato from this guy called Curtis's plants. He grows tomatoes for his girlfriend I guess. So I put a fence around my potatoes so no one could get one. Every day after work I came and gave some water to my potatoes. Most of my potatoes survived the high temperatures some of them died but Sam was right because he told me that I was gonna change the way that I think of the neighborhood from when I first came and he was right. With all the time that I spend in the garden I changed my mind about the neighborhood. The neighborhood was nice but you need to discover it your own way. But it was nice and very beautiful.

ESOL 3, GLEN BURNIE HIGH SCHOOL, 2015-2016

IMAGE BY: TEMA ENCARNACION

ESOL 3, GLEN BURNIE HIGH SCHOOL, 2015-2016

ABOUT ROSA

My name is Rosa. I'm from Mexico City and two and a half years ago I came here to Maryland for two reasons. The first reason was because Mexico has an extreme challenge. Not just because of the everyday things are wrong like people kill or steal, but because Mexico is not a safe place. It's my country and also has the best food and beautiful traditions. But these things can't make me see Mexico as a safe place. The other and last reason was because my mom's family lives here so my parents made a decision and we came here.

TO HEAR THE CHAPTER READ BY THE AUTHOR, SCAN THE QR CODE OR USE THE LINK BELOW.

tinyurl.com/rosaschapter

Rosa's Chapter

I really miss my beautiful culture, my good neighborhoods and my big city, but this decision was not bad. My name is Rosa. I'm from Mexico City, where you can have a nice community. I'm telling you that because everyone talks to you. Also one thing that I like is that we had everything close by, like grocery stores and malls. Our population is big in Mexico and the different states are so beautiful like Puebla, Toluca, Sonora, Chiapas, Costa Rica, Nayarit, San Luis Potosí, Baja California Sur, Baja California Norte, Chihuahua, etc, etc. Everything in my country was amazing.

Juanita and Teresa two old women were the best people with me and my family because they really loved my brother and me like we were their son and their daughter. And I appreciate that. That was my Mexico because after some days Mexico changed. Nobody could go outside just because many teenagers adopted the easy life. Now they are stealing things, other teenagers are addicted to drugs and other things and this was why we left Mexico. It was a difficult decision because my parents needed to get a good option for us. Before we moved my Mom's family lived in the United States, in Cleveland Heights where there are good workers and also they have a nice pay check. So my parents made a decision and then they chose to come to the United States because they think that this is the best decision.

After three months when finally we moved it was like getting something that tickled my stomach. We arrived in Cleveland Heights and it was amazing. Everybody was nice and they were making us feel so special. That was when many memories came back to my mind and I focused on my beautiful Mexico. When I came back again to the world and I put my foot on land and I left the memories just for one second, I thought about the big problem in my family. Everybody spoke English. We can just say like "Hi," "Good morning," "Thank you," and "No problem." We really have a problem because we don't speak English! After some days my brother and I went to school and I can say that was difficult for us. There were new friends, a new language and a new world. But our uncle was helping us to not be scared at wherever situation arose. One of his favorite phrases was "You can do it if you want." The school was fun. Some of our friends can speak Spanish and I think I like the school.

At the end of the school day, when we went back home, we saw an interesting garden with different types of plants. That was a big surprise because it was like a real life paradise, but Cesar, my brother, wanted to go close to see each plant. It was there when Cesar wanted to plant one flower to tell a story about us. In this moment we had an idea to plant our own flowers and get our own story and he said, "What if we plant an orchid flower?" I said "Why this type of plant?" And he said "We need to tell our story and also we miss Mexico because are our grandparents and our friends are there. I thought about everything and I needed to say Mexico is the best country. I wanted to go back!

Cesar was right, but I didn't want to say more words because I thought we would cry. The day was long and the weather was so nice. We needed to go to the store and buy the orchid flower. After we went to buy the flower, he went back to the place to plant the flower. After we got the materials to plant the flower we saw a young boy come to us. We got nervous because we thought about what he wanted and how we would answer him. But when he approached us he was speaking in Spanish and we knew he maybe was from Costa Rica or the Dominican Republic. He explained to us that he can speak the two languages because he is from Puerto Rico. Also he talked about the garden and the garden's history. He asked me about what I did with the flower and I can remember exactly what he said to me. He came to the garden telling me in Spanish "Hello how are you?" And I said, "I'm good what are about you?" "I'm well thank you, how do you see the garden do you like it?" "Yes its pretty its looks like paradise!" "Yes everybody thinks that and also says that, you are new in this neighborhood?" I responded, "Yes a couple days ago I came here." He asked, "Do you like it?" "Yes I like this neighborhood but the language is so difficult." He told me, "Don't worry this is a new start to your life and step by step you can learn to speak well. He asked if I wanted to plan my flower. Yes I wanted to. He asked, "Can I help you?" "Yes of course," I said. That was was when my brother and I had a new friend.

ABOUT KAFHER

My name is Kafher and I was born New York and then I moved to Glen Burnie. I came from New York to Glen Burnie because my parents did not want me to be a person that does drugs and alcohol so my mom and my dad moved to get far away from the New Yorkers and live a better life here.

While we were moving everything from New York to Glen Burnie we used my dad's truck to move all of our stuff to our new home while me and my mom were finding a house that had a garden and nice neighbors that come outside. Our neighbors asked if we were moving here and my mom said "Yes." They said, "Nice to meet you."

When we got everything to our new home we did not know a lot about the city so we tried to look for the nearest school. We looked and looked and my neighbor said there is one nearby. My mom and I went inside and I started on Monday. Later, we rode around to get used to the city and my mom said this is a better place for you.

In the story *Seedfolks* it relates with my story because one person inspires another then the whole community changes. In my story people looked at our garden and loved it and went to clean their yards or started to plant and our whole community changed.

ESOL 3, Glen Burnie High School, 2015-2016

Kafher's Chapter

When I was a child me and my family were staying in New York for a while but my family didn't like it there because school was a bad influence on me. So my mom said we're going to find a different place to live so we went to Cleveland. I was so shy because I didn't think I was going to get used to this city and their schools because they are full of people that I didn't even know. When I walked in school for the first day I was so shy and did not talk in school. The teacher said that we had to do rotations and while we were doing the rotations we had to say our names with the ball and talk about our life and I was so shy I didn't want to do the activity.

But a month later I got used to the city and I made friends that came to talk to me. We talked and became friends and when we came from New York we went to the house in a valley that was near my school. We looked for a house and we found the perfect house so that my mom would drop me off at school and she could go to work faster. When it was the weekend I went outside and rode my bike around my community for the first time. When I rode around it looked like a nice place to be living in. The community was a nice place to play around There were some people outside.

A kid called me over to play and when I was heading there his parents asked me if I was new around the community. I told them yes. They said, "I would like to get to know you and your family." I said, "Okay, you want me to get them." They said, "sure." So I went to get my family and then my parents came and were talking and I was with their children and we became friends. We had started to go over to each other's houses and play around. After my parents and his parents were talking about the community and they told my parents "If you go farther in the community there is a bad place for us to go. They told me not to ever go there. I said, "Okay, I will never go there. One day me and my father were walking around the community and my dad said, "Look you see that garden with all those vegetables?" He asked and I said "yes" and my dad asked if I wanted one in front of the house and I said, "Yes dad, please." So we went to the shed and he grabbed the shovel and made four holes and my mom went to buy seeds. While my mom was gone my dad was digging and he made four lines. Two were for the plants and the other two were for water so the plants have water to grow. My mom came home and gave us the seeds so my dad put the seeds in the hole and the sun came out the next day. I couldn't wait for our vegetables to grow so my mom could make food with many vegetables that were healthy from the garden. This way she does not need to go buy vegetables so she won't waste money at all for vegetables.

 While the plants were still growing our neighbors loved to water the plants. They came and she said she loved our garden and that she wanted to plant too. So they stayed for a while. Then the next day I saw her and her family growing plants and I went home and told my mom. She said that they really liked our garden so they did the same.

 I went to check my plants and they needed water so I went to turn the sprinkler on and I watered the plants The sun was bright and made them healthy and so we could get our healthy vegetables. The next few days I was in my house watching TV and some people from our neighborhood stopped and looked at our garden. I didn't know what they were saying so I pretended that I was going to water plants and they started to talk to me They wanted plants so I guess they went and made the garden. We were eating dinner and my parents were telling me that people saw our plants and they wanted a garden like ours. So soon the community was filled with gardens and I said they were inspired by us and I was so happy that people started to plant vegetables and to be a healthy community.

 The other day I told my dad to look at how the whole community changed with gardens and people were happy that they loved their garden.

My parents told me that there are people who don't care about the environment or gardening and others try to show people what would happen but they still won't care. But their are people that like the environment and they don't want it to end up dirty so then it won't be a clean and healthy world so people can plant their garden.

ABOUT EDWIN

My name is Edwin Alexander. I was born in El Salvador but I came to the United States when I was ten years old. Now I am nineteen. I came to America and went to Maryland because my mother lived in this state. After a while, I began to study in high school. Later I moved to Glen Burnie High School.

In the book *Seedfolks*, the character Nora cared for a man named Mr. Myles who is in a wheelchair. I learned from Mr. Myles and from Nora to never give up.

ESOL 3, GLEN BURNIE HIGH SCHOOL, 2015-2016

EDWIN'S CHAPTER

My name is Edwin and I am from El Salvador. My mother moved us to Cleveland Heights because she wanted a better job. My neighbors are good people and the community is quiet. I have no problems with my neighbors because where I live is peaceful.

One day I go to play soccer with my friends, like I do everyday. This particular day I found a garden.

To hear the chapter read by the author, scan the QR code or use the link below.

tinyurl.com/edwinschapter

ABOUT DAVID

I'm David and I am from El Salvador. I came to the United States because my dad was here and I have not seen him for a couple of years. I wanted to spend some time with him. When I got here in Glen Burnie on my first day I could not believe that I was here already and also I was sad because I didn't have any friends here. All of them were in El Salvador and I was missing them a lot.

The first day in Glen Burnie my family and I went to a restaurant called Qdoba and I was happy because I liked the food that they had in that restaurant. When I came here it was summer and the schools were closed. One month later school started again and it was time to go to school. My first day in school was sad because I didn't know anybody in the school. But days later I started to talk with some people and I made some friends and the school was getting interesting for me and I liked it.

Seedfolks is a book that talks about some people and their lives. All of them have something in common that and it is that they all plant something in the neighborhood and came to the garden to plant beans and other plants.

I relate Gonzalo's chapter in Seedfolk. Gonzalo's is similar to me because he moved to United States with his dad too and like Gonzalo said "The older you are, the younger you get when you move to the United States". I got older too because I had to learn English and help my dad when we go to a store to buy food or something.

ESOL 3, GLEN BURNIE HIGH SCHOOL, 2015-2016

DAVID'S CHAPTER

My Name is David and I came to the United States because my dad was here. He came here because he wanted to build a big house for us in El Salvador and he could not make enough money there so he decided to move here. After a couple of years my sisters and brother came too and then me. I hadn't seen him for a long time. I wanted to be with him and my brother and sisters too. My father had a job as a gardener full time near our house when I came here. Almost everyday I used to go to the pretty garden to try to help my old father a little.

In the beginning our neighborhood had some pretty big problems. One of those was a factory near the neighborhood. The factory was letting off smoke and the kids in the community were getting sick with breathing problems like asthma because the smoke was pretty bad. A few days later the people started to protest and then the government decided to close the factory. That was one problem resolved. The other one was that some people were being racist with Hispanic people. When I got to the United States I could not speak English well so I started to go to school and I made some friends. They was born here so they could speak English pretty good, but their parents were from my country. Those guys helped me to learn English and a few months later I was speaking English too.

One day I was walking to the garden where my father worked like I used to everyday and I saw Gonzalo walking by. He started to talk "Hi, how are you?" he asked. "I'm pretty good," I said. Gonzalo responded, "I saw your father the other day planting something in the garden. He said that you were going to plant something but I went to his garden just a few minutes ago and you did not plant anything." I said, "It is because I had too much homework to do the last few days, and I couldn't go to garden. But I will do it whenever I have chance." Gonzalo responded, "Okay." I said to him, "Okay, I have to go. Nice to see you." Gonzalo said, "Okay, nice to see you too".

ESOL 3, Glen Burnie High School, 2015-2016

So I went to the garden after that conversation with Gonzalo. My father was adding water in the garden, and I decided to help him a little. I planted something but I did not know what I wanted to plant, so in that moment I remembered that in my neighborhood there was a really cute girl that I liked and I wanted to give her something special.

I talked to her before and I asked her some questions. So I knew that her birthday was coming soon and I wanted to give her a present. So that's why I decided to plant roses because I knew that she loved roses. I planted the roses and about two weeks later my roses started to grow. Everyday in the morning I went to the garden and watered the roses and also in the evening after school. So one and a half months later my plants were ready. They were really beautiful. The red roses were her favorite color. Her birthday was one week later so they were ready almost the date that I wanted. Her birthday came and I gave her the roses, some chocolates and a big present, she was really happy because she did not know that I liked her.

To hear the chapter read by the author, scan the QR code or use the link below.

tinyurl.com/davidschapter

ESOL 3, GLEN BURNIE HIGH SCHOOL, 2015-2016

Image by: Christian

ESOL 3, GLEN BURNIE HIGH SCHOOL, 2015-2016

ABOUT CARLOS

My name is Carlos. I'm from El Salvador and I came here to Glen Burnie, in the United States because my parents were here and in El Salvador there are a lot of gangs.

My first day in Glen Burnie was good because I was so happy because finally I saw my parents after a long time. We went out to eat with my family. When I read *Seedfolks*, a book we read in my ESOL class, it made me remember when my grandpa planted tomatoes in El Salvador. When I read *Seedfolks* it made me feel good because it made me remember when I was in El Salvador.

ESOL 3, Glen Burnie High School, 2015-2016

Carlos' Chapter

When I was in El Salvador with my family my parents were here in the United States. My mom wanted me to move with her to the United states and I wanted to but i didn't want to leave my family in El Salvador because I didn't have an idea how it was going to be in this new place that i had never been before.

My mom told me that I had to go to school and I told her that I didn't want to go to school because I didn't speak any English and I was scared to go to new school that is so different than my old school. I couldn't speak the same language because it was too difficult for me. Where I lived was not bad. I lived in a house and there were not a lot people.

In the summer I planted tomatoes in the back of the house. I planted tomatoes because my mom told me to do it. It was really good for me because that made me remember my grandpa because he always planted tomatoes in El Salvador. I was with my mom and I told her that my grandpa always did that in El Salvador. My plants were growing in the garden really good. It looked really good there even though the neighborhood didn't look good. I will continue doing it in the summer because I want to show it to my grandpa because he will come this summer. I want him to see that I can do what he showed me to do. I just want him to be proud of me.

ABOUT THE AUTHORS

ESOL 3 is an intermediate level English language acquisition class for students learning English as a second, third or even fourth language. The students featured in this book come from many parts of the world and speak a variety of languages. They have varying educational backgrounds, English language proficiencies and have been in the United States from anywhere from a matter of months to several years. This ESOL class, like ones like it throughout the country, helps students learn English, but also provides a common experience for people representing different cultural backgrounds, religions and languages...just like the *Seedfolks* garden.